We hope
enjoy our book.

Sharkey + Susan

Sharkey Meets Kittyhead

Written by Susan R. Stoltz

Other Books by Susan R. Stoltz

The Part-Time Thief and Other Appraisal Stories

Short Stories by Susan R. Stoltz

"Old Blue"
"The Hunt - A Murder Well Deserved"
"All Was Calm"

Susan R. Stoltz

Sharkey Meets Kittyhead
The Adventures of Sharkey the Dog

Photography by
Susan R. Stoltz

Edited by
Elizabeth Zack

Library of Congress Cataloging-in-Publication Data
Library of Congress Control Number: 2010916676

ISBN 10: 1453859675

ISBN 13: 9781453859674

Printed in the United States of America

Paint Horse Press
United States of America

For Avelina and Emerson,
with all my love!

Sharkey has always lived with her mother, Charm, and Susan, her human, in a little house in the mountains.

There is a park just beyond the fence where they walk almost every day. Sometimes Sharkey barks at the people in the park.

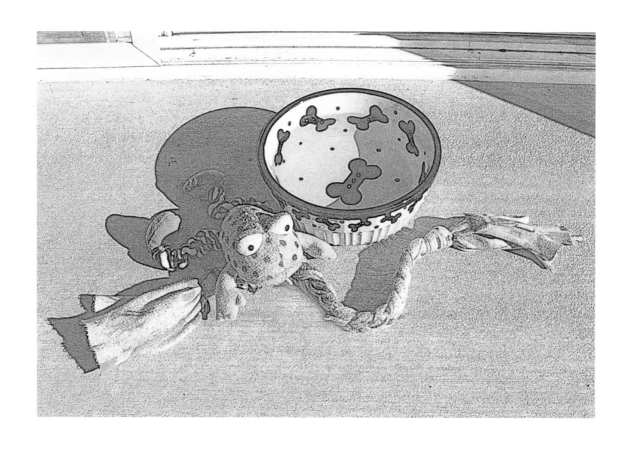

On the back steps is her
favorite bowl for water. The dish has
dog bones painted all the way around.
Sharkey has lots of toys.
Mr. Froggy squeaks
when she squeezes him.

Each morning begins in the very
same way. First there are cuddles
and hugs in the big bed.
Sometimes Sharkey licks Susan
on the face because she's so happy.
"Is it time for our morning bone?"
Susan asks in a cheerful voice.

There are bones of many flavors in the jar. Sharkey always hopes she will get one that tastes like cheese. This kind is her very favorite.

For Sharkey and Charm the days are filled with walks in the park, naps in the warm sunshine and playing with their toys. Sharkey likes to nap in her cozy bed the very best.

When she's outside,
Sharkey enjoys digging holes.
She smells the flowers, and
helps Susan with the gardening.

But most of all she likes to bark.
"Sharkey!"
Susan would scold.
"Quit barking so much!"

Sharkey would look so sad
that Susan would pick her up and
give her a big hug.

"You're the cutest little dog ever!"
she would say, as she gave her a
big kiss on the top of her head.

Susan could never be
angry for very long.

One day Susan came home with
a large crate.
It was the same
kind that Sharkey and Charm
slept in when they were away from
home. Something inside the crate
was making strange noises.

"Meow, meow, meow!" cried an unfamiliar voice.

Susan set the crate down. Sharkey and Charm went to see what might be inside.

"Just what I thought," said Charm as Susan opened the wire door. "A cat."

"A what?" asked Sharkey.

"I'm a cat," said the cat in a voice that had a whirring sound to it.

"What is your name, cat?" asked Charm. Before he could answer, Susan patted both dogs on the head and announced, "Sharkey, Charm, this is Kittyhead. He's going to be part of our family."

"What's a cat?" asked Sharkey.

"Cats," said Charm in her wise old way, "are different from dogs. Most cats I've met are friendly as long as you don't chase them."

At first Sharkey didn't like Kittyhead at all. Kittyhead drank out of Sharkey's favorite bowl. That made her angry.

Kittyhead played with her toys. That made her angry too.

"We are not the same," Sharkey growled at Kittyhead.
"Your ears stick up and mine fold down."

"That's true," the cat would purr.

"Your tail is long and mine is very short," Sharkey barked.

"That's true," Kittyhead meowed.

"Your eyes are blue and mine are brown," Sharkey whined.

"That's true," the cat replied. Kittyhead never said too much at once.

One day Kittyhead made Sharkey particularly angry. He slept in one of her favorite cozy places and wouldn't move. There was no room for Sharkey at all.

"I'm so mad at that cat! I wish he
never came to live with us.
We were just fine before
he got here," she cried.

"You know," Charm said
in her very calm way,
"I understand why you're angry, but
you and Kittyhead have more in
common than you realize."

"Like what?" Sharkey said in a voice
as angry as she could muster.
"There is nothing the same about
that cat and I!"

"Well," Charm continued, "you both like
to play outside in the yard, and you
both like to take naps in the sun."

"But he sleeps in my bed!"
Sharkey growled.

"You both have whiskers, and you both
have four white feet," Charm added.

"I don't care."

"You both like to gobble your dinner as fast as you can."

"So what," Sharkey said as she rolled in the grass. "I don't like him."

"Susan loves you both very much," Charm said as she found a spot to lie down. "She loves us even though we aren't the same."

"Just because you're different doesn't mean you can't be friends," Charm explained. "Perhaps Kittyhead is lonely and would like a good buddy. Why don't you try to be his friend and see what happens?"

So the next time Kittyhead
came to sit on the patio Sharkey
didn't shoo him away.

When Kittyhead sat down next to
Sharkey on the sofa, she moved over
to give him a bit of room.

Sharkey and Kittyhead learned that
there was enough space for both
of them in the cozy place
in the sun.

"Kittyhead might not be
so bad after all," she thought.

It wasn't long until they became good friends.

They shared the house and they played in the yard. They took naps in the sunshine and played with the toys.

Pretty soon Sharkey forgot
all about how different they were
and realized there were lots of
things they could do together.

"See," Charm said gently.
"You can learn to be happy even
though you aren't the same."

"That's true," meowed Kittyhead,
who never
said too much at once.

And with that he gave Sharkey a
big kiss on the top of her head!

Can you find the hidden bone
in this book?

It looks like this:

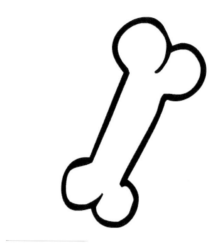

Here's a hint:
It might be big and it might be small.
It could be short or it could be tall.
Is it in the grass or on a wall?
Here is a hint: it's round like a ball.

For more about Sharkey and
her friends and to find out how
they are working to help
other animals in need,
visit her website:

www.Sharkeypup.com

A percentage of the profits from this book go to support other animals in need through'
Actors and Others for Animals.'

Here is some information about their organization.

ACTORS AND OTHERS FOR ANIMALS

11523 Burbank Boulevard
North Hollywood, CA 91601
Telephone: (818) 755-6045; (818) 755-6323; Fax: (818) 755-6048
Website: www.actorsandothers.com

Actors and Others for Animals is a nonprofit organization with a mission to eliminate pet overpopulation, ensure the care and protection of pet companions and improve the quality of life for economically challenged, disadvantaged and underserved pet guardians by providing referral and financial assistance for spay/neuter and veterinary medical procedures together with other animal/human bond enriching programs.

Founded in 1971 by the renowned actor Richard Basehart and his wife, Diana, Actors and Others utilized the celebrity status of early members to draw vital media attention to the plight of animals and influence needed change. Today, Actors and Others is still reshaping public awareness of animals with the help of celebrity members. JoAnne Worley currently serves as president, and board members include Betty White and Loretta Swit. *No celebrity is ever paid to appear on behalf of Actors and Others. They enthusiastically use their media appeal to educate, inform and enlighten the public about animals in crisis.*

Actors and Others has taken another step in its quest to eliminate pet overpopulation by launching *SpayCalifornia*, a state-wide referral network/database that connects pet guardians throughout the State of California (via internet and telephone) with participating programs and veterinarians offering low-cost services. The website www.spaycalifornia.org, receives over 100 hits per day!

Actors and Others' many other programs include: (1) providing financial subsidies for emergency medical procedures; (2) providing education and assistance on how to trap, alter, return and care for stray cats through its feral cat program; (3) introducing future generations to animal awareness and responsible pet care through its humane education classes; (3) providing comfort to patients in local nursing homes and hospitals through its growing pet assisted therapy program; and, (4) distributing donated pet food to those who find themselves in need of a "helping hand" when available.

Reading is fun
Just take a good look,
Even Sharkey enjoys
A really good book!

You can have great adventures
And go anywhere,
You can even find people
That have purple hair!

So sit down and read
One each to the other,
A poem or story
To your sister or brother!

~ Sharkey

Made in the USA
Charleston, SC
28 January 2011